Ladybird I'm
Ready...to Sing!

Illustrated by Sonia Esplugas

Old MacDonald had a Farm

Old MacDonald had a farm, E I E I O,
And on that farm he had a cow, E I E I O.
With a moo-moo here and a moo-moo there,
Here a moo, there a moo, everywhere a moo-moo.
Old MacDonald had a farm, E I E I O.

Old MacDonald had a farm, E I E I O,
And on that farm he had a sheep, E I E I O.
With a baa-baa here and a baa-baa there,
Here a baa, there a baa, everywhere a baa-baa.
Old MacDonald had a farm, E I E I O.

Old MacDonald had a farm, E I E I O,
And on that farm he had a pig, E I E I O.
With an oink-oink here and an oink-oink there,
Here an oink, there an oink, everywhere an oink-oink.
Old MacDonald had a farm, E I E I O.

Old MacDonald had a farm, E I E I O,
And on his farm he had a duck, E I E I O.
With a quack-quack here and a quack-quack there,
Here a quack, there a quack, everywhere a quack-quack.
Old MacDonald had a farm, E I E I O.

Old MacDonald had a farm, E I E I O,
And on that farm he had a horse, E I E I O.
With a neigh-neigh here and a neigh-neigh there,
Here a neigh, there a neigh, everywhere a neigh-neigh.
Old MacDonald had a farm, E I E I O.

The House that Jack Built

This is the house that Jack built!
This is the malt that lay in the house that Jack built.
This is the rat that ate the malt,
That lay in the house that Jack built.

This is the cat that killed the rat,
That ate the malt that lay in the house that Jack built.
This is the dog that worried the cat,
That killed the rat that ate the malt,
That lay in the house that Jack built.

This is the cow with the crumpled horn,
That tossed the dog that worried the cat,
That killed the rat that ate the malt,
That lay in the house that Jack built.

This is the maiden all forlorn,
That milked the cow with the crumpled horn,
That tossed the dog that worried the cat,
That killed the rat that ate the malt,
That lay in the house that Jack built.

This is the man all tattered and torn,
That kissed the maiden all forlorn,
That milked the cow with the crumpled horn,
That tossed the dog that worried the cat,
That killed the rat that ate the malt,
That lay in the house that Jack built.

This is the priest all shaven and shorn,
That married the man all tattered and torn,
That kissed the maiden all forlorn,
That milked the cow with the crumpled horn,
That tossed the dog that worried the cat,
That killed the rat that ate the malt,
That lay in the house that Jack built.

This is the cock that crowed in the morn,
That woke the priest all shaven and shorn,
That married the man all tattered and torn,
That kissed the maiden all forlorn,
That milked the cow with the crumpled horn,
That tossed the dog that worried the cat,
That killed the rat that ate the malt,
That lay in the house that Jack built.

This is the farmer sowing his corn,
That kept the cock that crowed in the morn,
That woke the priest all shaven and shorn,
That married the man all tattered and torn,
That kissed the maiden all forlorn,
That milked the cow with the crumpled horn,
That tossed the dog that worried the cat,
That killed the rat that ate the malt,
That lay in the house that Jack built!

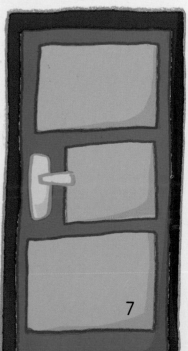

The Wheels on the Bus

The wheels on the bus go round and round,
Round and round, round and round,
The wheels on the bus go round and round,
All day long.

The wipers on the bus go swish-swish-swish,
Swish-swish-swish, swish-swish-swish,
The wipers on the bus go swish-swish-swish,
All day long.

The horn on the bus goes beep-beep-beep,
Beep-beep-beep, beep-beep-beep,
The horn on the bus goes beep beep beep,
All day long.

The children on the bus go up and down,
Up and down, up and down,
The children on the bus go up and down,
All day long.

The babies on the bus go wah-wah-wah,
Wah-wah-wah, wah-wah-wah,
The babies on the bus go wah-wah-wah,
All day long.

The mums on the bus go ssh-ssh-ssh,
Ssh-ssh-ssh, ssh-ssh-ssh,
The mums on the bus go ssh-ssh-ssh,
All day long.

London Bridge is Falling Down

London Bridge is falling down,
Falling down, falling down,
London Bridge is falling down,
My fair lady.

Row, Row, Row Your Boat

Row, row, row your boat,
Gently down the stream,
Merrily, merrily, merrily, merrily,
Life is but a dream.

Row, row, row your boat,
Gently down the stream,
If you see a crocodile,
Don't forget to scream —

Arghh!

There Was an Old Lady Who Swallowed a Fly

There was an old lady who swallowed a fly;
I don't know why she swallowed a fly –
Perhaps she'll die!

There was an old lady who swallowed a spider,
That wriggled and wiggled and jiggled inside her;
She swallowed the spider to catch the fly;
I don't know why she swallowed a fly –
Perhaps she'll die!

There was an old lady who swallowed a bird,
How absurd to swallow a bird!
She swallowed the bird to catch the spider,
She swallowed the spider to catch the fly;
I don't know why she swallowed a fly –
Perhaps she'll die!

There was an old lady who swallowed a cat,
Fancy that to swallow a cat!
She swallowed the cat to catch the bird,
She swallowed the bird to catch the spider,
She swallowed the spider to catch the fly;
I don't know why she swallowed a fly –
Perhaps she'll die!

There was an old lady that swallowed a dog,
What a hog, to swallow a dog!
She swallowed the dog to catch the cat,
She swallowed the cat to catch the bird,
She swallowed the bird to catch the spider,
She swallowed the spider to catch the fly;
I don't know why she swallowed a fly –
Perhaps she'll die!

There was an old lady who swallowed a cow,
I don't know how she swallowed a cow!
She swallowed the cow to catch the dog,
She swallowed the dog to catch the cat,
She swallowed the cat to catch the bird,
She swallowed the bird to catch the spider,
She swallowed the spider to catch the fly;
I don't know why she swallowed a fly –
Perhaps she'll die!

There was an old lady who swallowed a horse...

She's dead, of course!

Ten in the Bed

There were ten in the bed and the little one said,
"Roll over! Roll over!"
So they all rolled over and one fell out.

There were nine in the bed and the little one said,
"Roll over! Roll over!"
So they all rolled over and one fell out.

There were eight in the bed and the little one said,
"Roll over! Roll over!"
So they all rolled over and one fell out.

There were seven in the bed and the little one said,
"Roll over! Roll over!"
So they all rolled over and one fell out.

There were six in the bed and the little one said,
"Roll over! Roll over!"
So they all rolled over and one fell out.

There were five in the bed and the little one said,
"Roll over! Roll over!"
So they all rolled over and one fell out.

There were four in the bed and the little one said,
"Roll over! Roll over!"
So they all rolled over and one fell out.

There were three in the bed and the little one said,
"Roll over! Roll over!"
So they all rolled over and one fell out.

There were two in the bed and the little one said,
"Roll over! Roll over!"
So they all rolled over and one fell out.

There was one in the bed and the little one said,
"Good night!"

If You're Happy
and You Know it

If you're happy and you know it clap your hands.
If you're happy and you know it clap your hands.
If you're happy and you know it and you really want to show it,
If you're happy and you know it clap your hands.

If you're happy and you know it stomp your feet.
If you're happy and you know it stomp your feet.
If you're happy and you know it and you really want to show it,
If you're happy and you know it stomp your feet.

If you're happy and you know it shout, "Hooray!"
If you're happy and you know it shout, "Hooray!"
If you're happy and you know it and you really want to show it,
If you're happy and you know it shout, "Hooray!"

If you're happy and you know it do all three.
If you're happy and you know it do all three.
If you're happy and you know it and you really want to show it,
If you're happy and you know it do all three!

Wind the Bobbin Up

Wind the bobbin up,
Wind the bobbin up.
Pull, pull,
Clap, clap, clap.
Wind it back again,
Wind it back again.
Pull, pull,
Clap, clap, clap.

Point to the ceiling,
Point to the floor,
Point to the window,
Point to the door.
Clap your hands together,
One, two, three.
Put your hands
Upon your knee.

Five Little Speckled Frogs

Five little speckled frogs,
Sat on a speckled log,
Eating some most delicious bugs
yum, yum!

One jumped into the pool,
Where it was nice and cool,
Then there were four speckled frogs
glug, glug!

Four little speckled frogs,
Sat on a speckled log,
Eating some most delicious bugs
yum, yum!

One jumped into the pool,
Where it was nice and cool,
Then there were three speckled frogs
glug, glug!

Three little speckled frogs,
Sat on a speckled log,
Eating some most delicious bugs
yum, yum!

One jumped into the pool,
Where it was nice and cool,
Then there were two speckled frogs
glug, glug!

Two little speckled frogs,
Sat on a speckled log,
Eating some most delicious bugs
yum, yum!

One jumped into the pool,
Where it was nice and cool,
Then there was one speckled frog
glug, glug!

One little speckled frog,
Sat on a speckled log,
Eating some most delicious bugs
yum, yum!

He jumped into the pool,
Where it was nice and cool,

Then there were **no** speckled frogs.

One Man Went to Mow

One man went to mow, went to mow a meadow.
One man and his dog,
Woof!
Went to mow a meadow.

Two men went to mow, went to mow a meadow,
Two men, one man and his dog,
Woof!
Went to mow a meadow.

Three men went to mow, went to mow a meadow,
Three men, two men, one man and his dog,
Woof!
Went to mow a meadow.

Four men went to mow, went to mow a meadow,
Four men, three men, two men, one man and his dog,
Woof!
Went to mow a meadow.

Five men went to mow, went to mow a meadow,
Five men, four men, three men, two men, one man and his dog,
Woof!
Went to mow a meadow.

This Old Man

This old man, he played one,
He played knick-knack on my thumb;
With a knick-knack paddy whack give a dog a bone,
This old man came rolling home.

This old man, he played two,
He played knick-knack on my shoe;
With a knick-knack paddy whack give a dog a bone,
This old man came rolling home.

This old man, he played three,
He played knick-knack on my knee;
With a knick-knack paddy whack give a dog a bone,
This old man came rolling home.

This old man, he played four,
He played knick-knack on the floor;
With a knick-knack paddy whack give a dog a bone,
This old man came rolling home.

This old man, he played five,
He played knick-knack on my hive;
With a knick-knack paddy whack give a dog a bone,
This old man came rolling home.

This old man, he played six,
He played knick-knack on some sticks;
With a knick-knack paddy whack give a dog a bone,
This old man came rolling home.

This old man, he played seven,
He played knick-knack up in heaven;
With a knick-knack paddy whack give a dog a bone,
This old man came rolling home.

This old man, he played eight,
He played knick-knack at my gate;
With a knick-knack paddy whack give a dog a bone,
This old man came rolling home.

This old man, he played nine,
He played knick-knack on my spine;
With a knick-knack paddy whack give a dog a bone,
This old man came rolling home.

This old man, he played ten,
He played knick-knack once again;
With a knick-knack paddy whack give a dog a bone,
This old man came rolling home.

Five Little Monkeys

Five little monkeys jumping on the bed,
One fell off and bumped his head.
Mummy called the doctor and the doctor said,
"No more monkeys jumping on the bed!"

Four little monkeys jumping on the bed,
One fell off and bumped her head.
Mummy called the doctor and the doctor said,
"No more monkeys jumping on the bed!"

Three little monkeys jumping on the bed,
One fell off and bumped his head.
Mummy called the doctor and the doctor said,
"No more monkeys jumping on the bed!"

Two little monkeys jumping on the bed,
One fell off and bumped her head.
Mummy called the doctor and the doctor said,
"No more monkeys jumping on the bed!"

One little monkey jumping on the bed,
He fell off and bumped his head.
Mummy called the doctor and the doctor said,
"Put those monkeys straight to bed!"

Incy Wincy Spider

Incy Wincy spider climbed up the waterspout,
Down came the rain and washed the spider out,
Out came the sun and dried up all the rain,
So Incy Wincy spider climbed up the spout again.

Down in the Jungle

Down in the jungle
Where nobody goes,
There's a great big gorilla
Washing his clothes.
With a rub-a-dub here,
A rub-a-dub there,
That's the way he washes his clothes.
Diddle-I-Dee, a boogie boogie woogie,
Diddle-I-Dee, a boogie boogie woogie,
Diddle-I-Dee, a boogie boogie woogie,
That's the way he washes his clothes.

Down in the jungle
Where nobody goes,
There's a slithery snake
Washing his clothes.
With a rub-a-dub here,
A rub-a-dub there,
That's the way he washes his clothes.
Diddle-I-Dee, a boogie boogie woogie,
Diddle-I-Dee, a boogie boogie woogie,
Diddle-I-Dee, a boogie boogie woogie,
That's the way he washes his clothes.

Down in the jungle
Where nobody goes,
There's a great big crocodile
Washing his clothes.
With a rub-a-dub here,
A rub-a-dub there,
That's the way he washes his clothes.
Diddle-I-Dee, a boogie boogie woogie,
Diddle-I-Dee, a boogie boogie woogie,
Diddle-I-Dee, a boogie boogie woogie,
That's the way he washes his clothes.

Down in the jungle
Where nobody goes,
There's a great big elephant
Washing his clothes.
With a rub-a-dub here,
A rub-a-dub there,
That's the way he washes his clothes.
Diddle-I-Dee, a boogie boogie woogie,
Diddle-I-Dee, a boogie boogie woogie,
Diddle-I-Dee, a boogie boogie woogie,
That's the way he washes his clothes.

Five Little Men in a Flying Saucer

Five little men in a flying saucer,
Flew round the world one day.
They looked left and right,
But they didn't like the sight,
So one man flew away.
Zoooooooooooom!

Four little men in a flying saucer,
Flew round the world one day.
They looked left and right,
But they didn't like the sight,
So one man flew away.
Zoooooooooooom!

Three little men in a flying saucer,
Flew round the world one day.
They looked left and right,
But they didn't like the sight,
So one man flew away.
Zooooooooooom!

Two little men in a flying saucer,
Flew round the world one day.
They looked left and right,
But they didn't like the sight,
So one man flew away.
Zooooooooooom!

One little man in a flying saucer,
Flew round the world one day.
He looked left and right,
But he didn't like the sight,
So that man flew away.
ZOOOOOOOOOOM!

Ten Fat Sausages

Ten fat sausages sizzling in a pan,
One went pop and the other went **BANG!**

Eight fat sausages sizzling in a pan,
One went pop and the other went **BANG!**

Six fat sausages sizzling in a pan,
One went pop and the other went **BANG!**

Four fat sausages sizzling in a pan,
One went pop and the other went **BANG!**

Two fat sausages sizzling in a pan,
One went pop and the other went **BANG!**

No fat sausages sizzling in the pan,
But all of a sudden the pan went **BANG!**

It went **BANG! BANG! BANG!**
Now there are no fat sausages
And no frying pan!

Jelly on a Plate

Jelly on a plate!
Jelly on a plate!
Wibble-wobble,
Wibble-wobble,
Jelly on a plate!

Candles on a cake!
Candles on a cake!
Blow them out,
Blow them out,
Candles on a cake!

Sweeties in a jar!
Sweeties in a jar!
Shake them up,
Shake them up,
Sweeties in a jar!

31

Sleeping Bunnies

See the bunnies sleeping till it's nearly noon.
Shall we wake them with a merry tune?
They're so still, are they ill?
Wake up little bunnies!
Hop little bunnies, hop, hop, hop.
Hop, hop, hop; hop, hop, hop.
Hop little bunnies, hop, hop, hop.
Hop, hop, hop...

See the bunnies sleeping till it's nearly noon.
Shall we wake them with a merry tune?
They're so still, are they ill?
Wake up little bunnies!
Skip little bunnies, skip, skip, skip.
Skip, skip, skip; skip, skip, skip.
Skip little bunnies, skip, skip, skip,
Skip, skip, skip...

See the bunnies sleeping till it's nearly noon.
Shall we wake them with a merry tune?
They're so still, are they ill?
Wake up little bunnies!
Jump little bunnies, jump, jump, jump.
Jump, jump, jump; jump, jump, jump.
Jump little bunnies, jump, jump, jump
Jump, jump, jump...

Hop little bunnies, hop, hop, hop,
Hop, hop, hop, hop, hop, hop.
Hop little bunnies, hop, hop, hop,
Hop, hop, hop!

The Farmer's in his Den

The farmer's in his den,
The farmer's in his den,
Eee-eye addy-oh,
The farmer's in his den.

The farmer wants a wife,
The farmer wants a wife,
Eee-eye addy-oh,
The farmer wants a wife.

The wife wants a child,
The wife wants a child,
Eee-eye addy-oh,
The wife wants a child.

The child wants a dog,
The child wants a dog,
Eee-eye addy-oh,
The child wants a dog.

The dog wants a bone,
The dog wants a bone,
Eee-eye addy-oh,
The dog wants a bone.

We all pat the dog,
We all pat the dog,
Eee-eye addy-oh,
We all pat the dog.

One Finger, One Thumb

One finger, one thumb,
keep moving.
One finger, one thumb,
keep moving.
We all stay merry and bright.

One finger, one thumb, one arm,
keep moving.
One finger, one thumb, one arm,
keep moving.
We all stay merry and bright.

One finger, one thumb, one arm, one leg,
keep moving.
One finger, one thumb, one arm, one leg,
keep moving.
We all stay merry and bright.

One finger, one thumb, one arm, one leg,
stand up, sit down, keep moving.
One finger, one thumb, one arm, one leg,
stand up, sit down, keep moving.
We all stay merry and bright.

Five Little Ducks

Five little ducks
Went swimming one day,
Over the hills and far away.
Mother Duck said,
"Quack, quack, quack, quack."
But only four little ducks came back.

Four little ducks
Went swimming one day,
Over the hills and far away.
Mother Duck said,
"Quack, quack, quack, quack."
But only three little ducks came back.

Three little ducks
Went swimming one day,
Over the hills and far away.
Mother Duck said,
"Quack, quack, quack, quack."
But only two little ducks came back.

Two little ducks
Went swimming one day,
Over the hills and far away.
Mother Duck said,
"Quack, quack, quack, quack."
But only one little duck came back.

One little duck
Went swimming one day,
Over the hills and far away.
Mother Duck said,
"Quack, quack, quack, quack."
And five little ducks came swimming back.

Baa, Baa, Black Sheep

Baa, baa, black sheep,
Have you any wool?
Yes sir, yes sir,
Three bags full.

One for the master,
One for the dame,
And one for the little boy
Who lives down the lane.

Here We Go Round the Mulberry Bush

Here we go round the mulberry bush,
The mulberry bush, the mulberry bush.
Here we go round the mulberry bush,
On a cold and frosty morning.

This is the way we wash our hands,
Wash our hands, wash our hands.
This is the way we wash our hands,
On a cold and frosty morning.

This is the way we wash our face,
Wash our face, wash our face.
This is the way we wash our face,
On a cold and frosty morning.

This is the way we brush our teeth,
Brush our teeth, brush our teeth.
This is the way we brush our teeth,
On a cold and frosty morning.

This is the way we comb our hair,
Comb our hair, comb our hair.
This is the way we comb our hair,
On a cold and frosty morning.

The Ants Go Marching

The ants go marching one by one.
Hoorah! Hoorah!
The ants go marching one by one.
Hoorah! Hoorah!
The ants go marching one by one;
The little one stops to suck his thumb,
And they all go marching down into the ground
To get out of the rain.

Boom! Boom! Boom! Boom!

The ants go marching two by two.
Hoorah! Hoorah!
The ants go marching two by two.
Hoorah! Hoorah!
The ants go marching two by two;
The little one stops to tie his shoe,
And they all go marching down into the ground
To get out of the rain.

Boom! Boom! Boom! Boom!

The ants go marching three by three.
Hoorah! Hoorah!
The ants go marching three by three.
Hoorah! Hoorah!
The ants go marching three by three;
The little one stops to climb a tree,
And they all go marching down into the ground
To get out of the rain.
Boom! Boom! Boom! Boom!

The ants go marching four by four.
Hoorah! Hoorah!
The ants go marching four by four.
Hoorah! Hoorah!
The ants go marching four by four;
The little one stops to shut the door,
And they all go marching down into the ground
To get out of the rain.
Boom! Boom! Boom! Boom!

The ants go marching five by five.
Hoorah! Hoorah!
The ants go marching five by five.
Hoorah! Hoorah!
The ants go marching five by five;
The little one stops to take a dive,
And they all go marching down into the ground
To get out of the rain.
Boom! Boom! Boom! Boom!

The Grand Old Duke of York

The grand old Duke of York,
He had ten thousand men,
He marched them up to the top of the hill,
And he marched them down again.

When they were up, they were up,
And when they were down, they were down,
And when they were only halfway up,
They were neither up nor down.

Humpty Dumpty

Humpty Dumpty sat on a wall,
Humpty Dumpty had a great fall;
All the King's horses and all the King's men,
Couldn't put Humpty together again.

Head, Shoulders, Knees and Toes

Head, shoulders, knees and toes,
Knees and toes.
Head, shoulders, knees and toes,
Knees and toes.
And eyes and ears and mouth and nose,
Head, shoulders, knees and toes,
Knees and toes.

Twinkle, Twinkle, Little Star

Twinkle, twinkle, little star,
How I wonder what you are.
Up above the world so high,
Like a diamond in the sky,
Twinkle, twinkle, little star,
How I wonder what you are.

Index of first lines